相撲 キティ

There are many wise and beautiful sayings.

One of them is "A journey of a thousand miles begins with the first step."

That means big things start small.

Another one is "Even monkeys fall from trees."

That means even experts make mistakes.

But the one that means the most to me is "Fall down seven times; get up eight."

It means never give up.

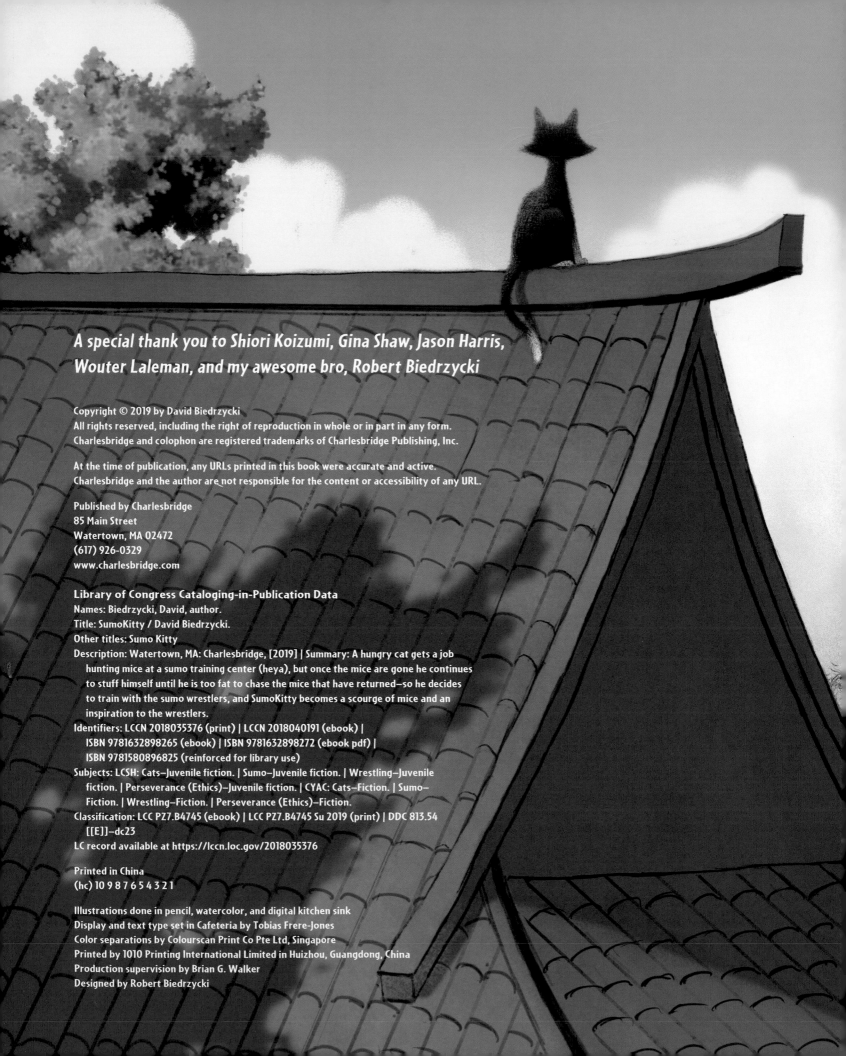

A special thank you to Shiori Koizumi, Gina Shaw, Jason Harris,
Wouter Laleman, and my awesome bro, Robert Biedrzycki

Published by Charlesbridge
85 Main Street
Watertown, MA 02472
(617) 926-0329
www.charlesbridge.com

Library of Congress Cataloging-in-Publication Data
Names: Biedrzycki, David, author.
Title: SumoKitty / David Biedrzycki.
Other titles: Sumo Kitty
Description: Watertown, MA: Charlesbridge, [2019] | Summary: A hungry cat gets a job
    hunting mice at a sumo training center (heya), but once the mice are gone he continues
    to stuff himself until he is too fat to chase the mice that have returned—so he decides
    to train with the sumo wrestlers, and SumoKitty becomes a scourge of mice and an
    inspiration to the wrestlers.
Identifiers: LCCN 2018035376 (print) | LCCN 2018040191 (ebook) |
    ISBN 9781632898265 (ebook) | ISBN 9781632898272 (ebook pdf) |
    ISBN 9781580896825 (reinforced for library use)
Subjects: LCSH: Cats—Juvenile fiction. | Sumo—Juvenile fiction. | Wrestling—Juvenile
    fiction. | Perseverance (Ethics)—Juvenile fiction. | CYAC: Cats—Fiction. | Sumo—
    Fiction. | Wrestling—Fiction. | Perseverance (Ethics)—Fiction.
Classification: LCC PZ7.B4745 (ebook) | LCC PZ7.B4745 Su 2019 (print) | DDC 813.54
    [[E]]—dc23
LC record available at https://lccn.loc.gov/2018035376

Printed in China
(hc) 10 9 8 7 6 5 4 3 2 1

Illustrations done in pencil, watercolor, and digital kitchen sink
Display and text type set in Cafeteria by Tobias Frere-Jones
Color separations by Colourscan Print Co Pte Ltd, Singapore
Printed by 1010 Printing International Limited in Huizhou, Guangdong, China
Production supervision by Brian G. Walker
Designed by Robert Biedrzycki

SumoKitty

DAVID BIEDRZYCKI

Charlesbridge

Sumo wrestlers don't like to give up.

gyōji (gyoh-jee): referee

In Japan they are known as rikishi, gentlemen of strength and honor.

rikishi (ree-kee-shee): wrestler

dohyō (doh-hyoh): ring

The champion rikishi
is called the yokozuna.
He's the best of the best.
When he enters the ring, called
the dohyō, he lifts his leg and
stomps his foot.

*yokozuna
(yoh-koh-zoo-nah):
grand champion*

*keshō-mawashi
(keh-shoh
mah-wah-shee):
ceremonial apron
worn before a
sumo match*

The crowd goes wild.

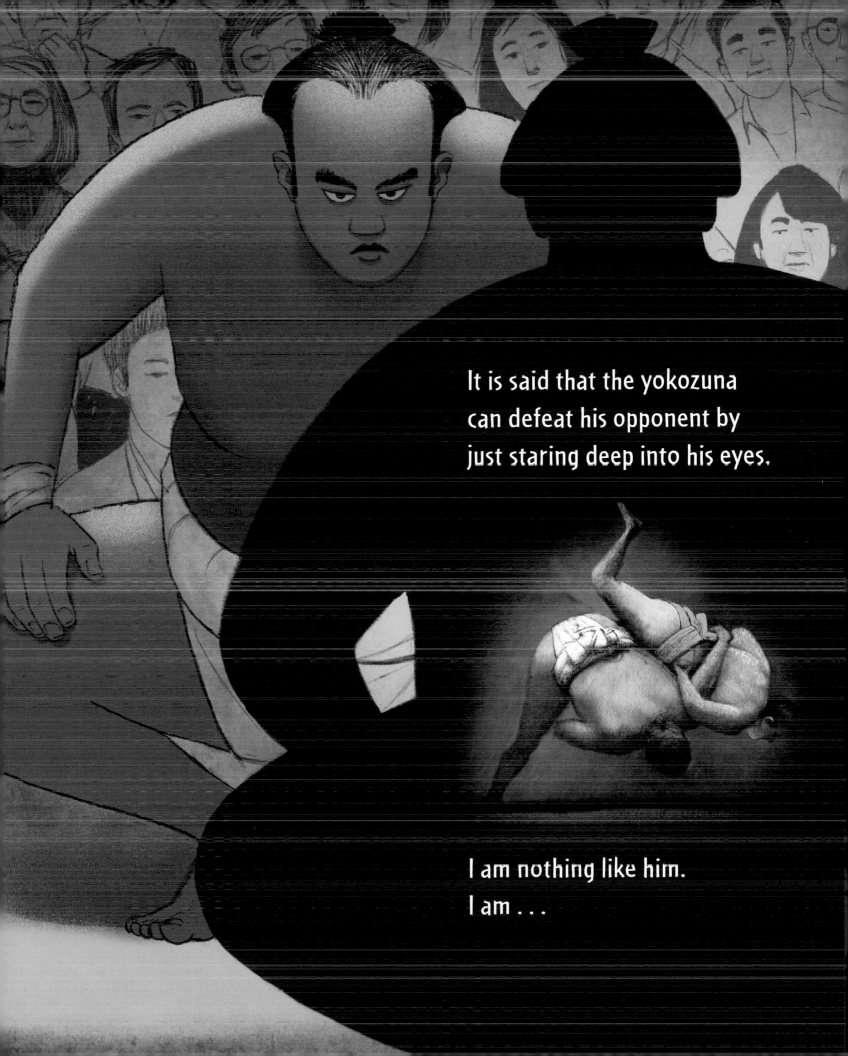

a kitty.

A hungry
stray kitty.

I will go
anywhere
for food.

I especially like following rikishi
back to their heya,
the place where they
practice, sleep, and . . .

heya (hay-yah): training center

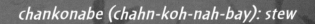
chankonabe (chahn-koh-nah-bay): stew

EAT!
Each meal is a feast.
Twice a day sumo wrestlers eat
a big stew called chankonabe.
It's made with everything I love.

Purr-fect for a stray cat like me.

I had it made in the heya until . . .

I was caught by the one they call Okamisan.
"So, you're the one who's been stealing our food," she said.
"If I ever catch you here again, I'll—"

okamisan (oh-kah-mee-sahn): manager of the heya

Over . . .

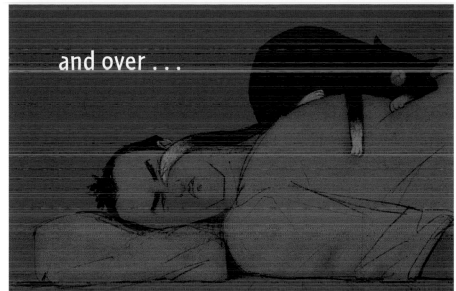

and over . . .

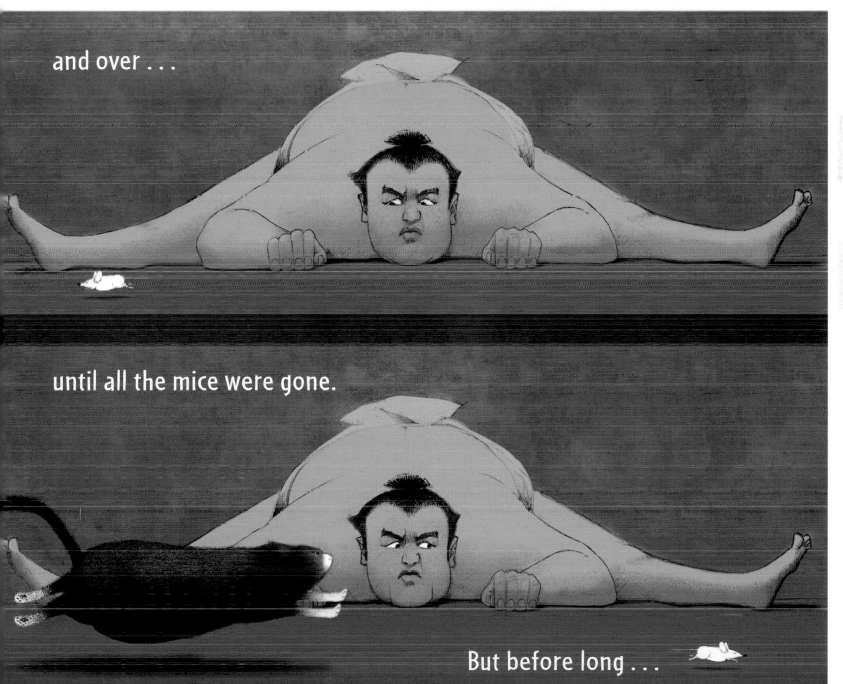

and over . . .

until all the mice were gone.

But before long . . .

all that eating started to show.

Kuma ate a lot, too.
But he moved
like a big,
powerful cat.

The ground shook
when he practiced.

shiko (shee-koh): leg stomp

Life was good in the heya.

We were one big,
happy family

until one day
I noticed . . .

The mice had made a comeback.

They were all over the kitchen. And they were laughing at me.

How dare they!

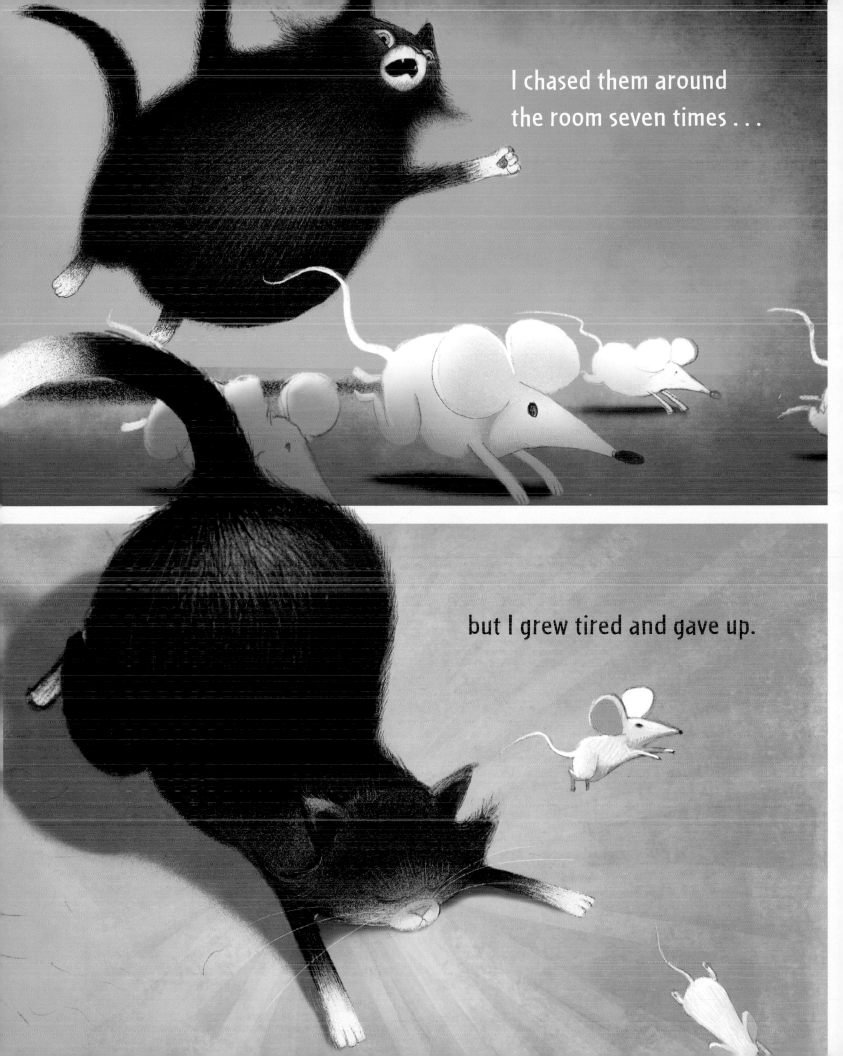

I chased them around
the room seven times . . .

but I grew tired and gave up.

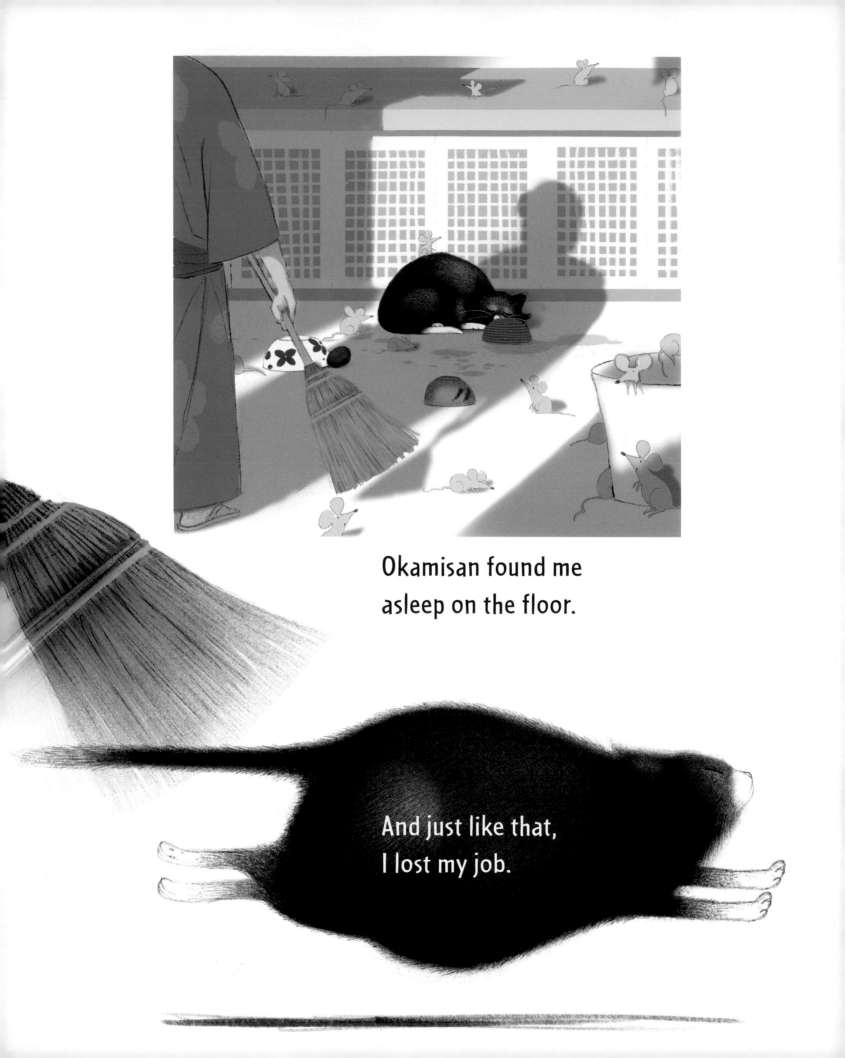

Okamisan found me
asleep on the floor.

And just like that,
I lost my job.

The next evening when all was quiet,
Kuma let me back inside.

He told me another wise saying.
"After the rain, the earth hardens," he said.

"When life gets tough, Kitty, it makes you stronger."

Kuma looked up at the picture of the yokozuna.
"I have fallen seven times to him," he said.

"He has humbled me the same way
the mice have humbled you, Kitty."

He put me outside with leftover stew and another saying:
"The cat that does not cry catches the mouse."

The next day I watched Kuma's every move.

When he stretched, I stretched.

When he did yoga, I did yoga.

When he attacked the teppo,
I attacked my scratching post.

teppo (tep-po): striking post

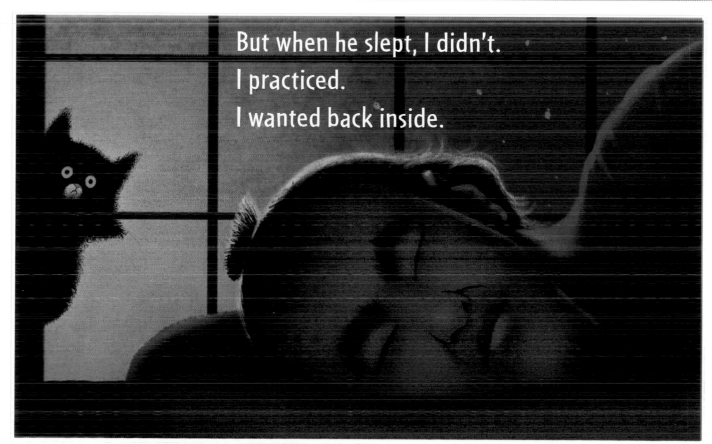

But when he slept, I didn't.
I practiced.
I wanted back inside.

I got my chance one night
as the rikishi were stretching.

A giant mouse stood in
the middle of the dohyō.

Before anyone saw him,
I leaped in and made my move.

Kuma and the others watched as I charged the mouse with a tachi-ai,

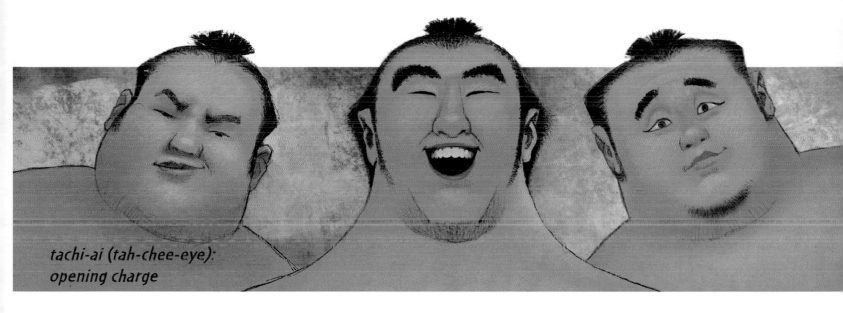

tachi-ai (tah-chee-eye):
opening charge

followed by a gaburi-yori.

gaburi-yori (gah-boo-ree-yoh-ree):
pushing move with the torso

I finished him off with a tsukidashi.

tsukidashi (tsoo-kee-dah-shee):
pushing move with the hands

More mice appeared.

They were no match for me.

I tossed them out of the dohyō and away from the heya for good.

And that
is how . . .

I became known as . . .

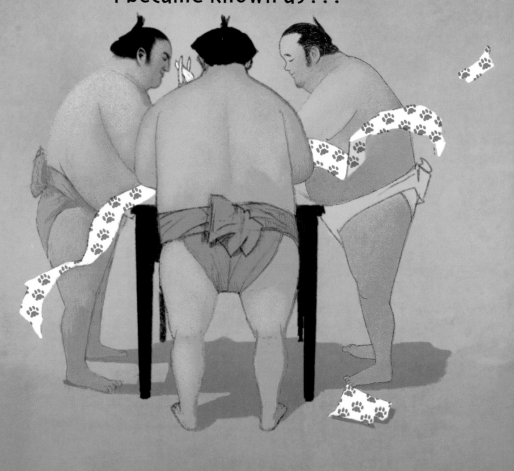

The next week I was given the best seat
at the basho, the sumo tournament.
Kuma did well, and he made it to the
final match.

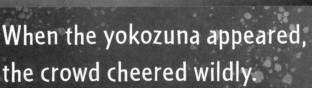

When the yokozuna appeared,
the crowd cheered wildly.

basho (bah-shoh): tournament

The yokozuna had mice sewn
on his mawashi.
Kuma was terrified of mice!

mawashi (mah-wah-shee): loincloth

To him, the yokozuna must have seemed as scary as
the giant mouse in our dohyō.

But then Kuma looked at me and shook his head. His face changed into the face of a warrior.

Kuma charged the yokozuna the same way
I charged the giant mouse.

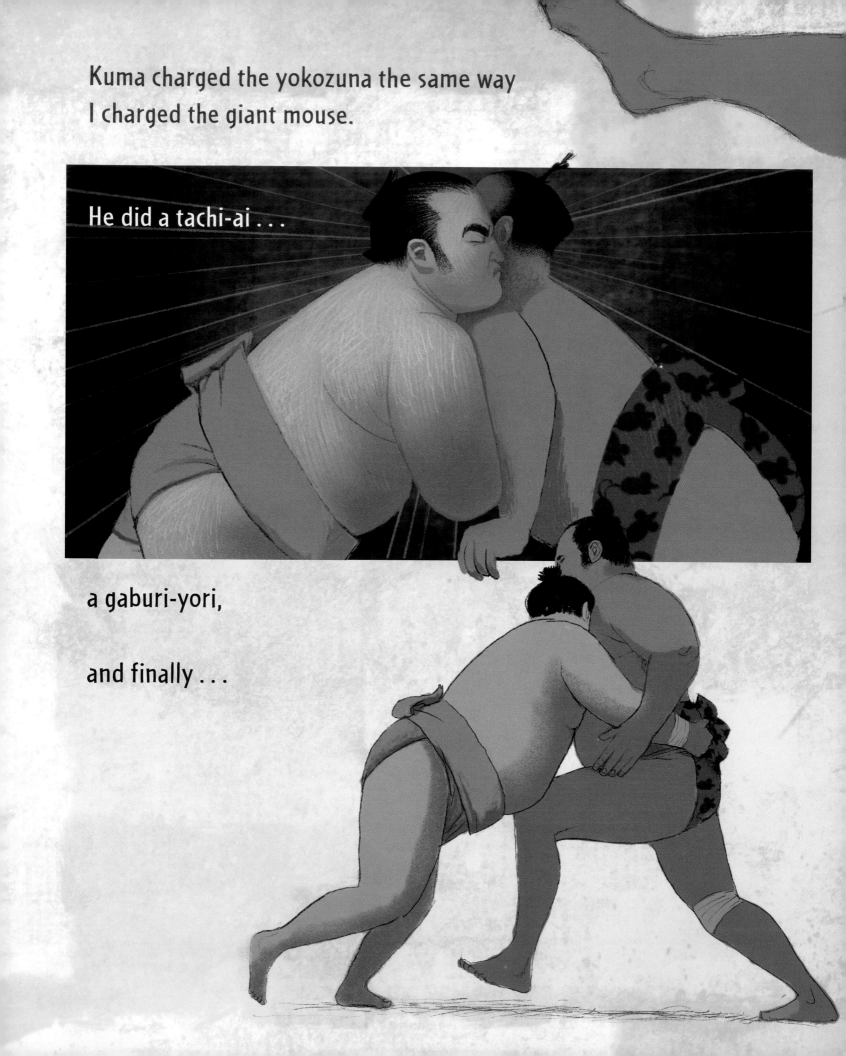

He did a tachi-ai . . .

a gaburi-yori,

and finally . . .

a tsukidashi.

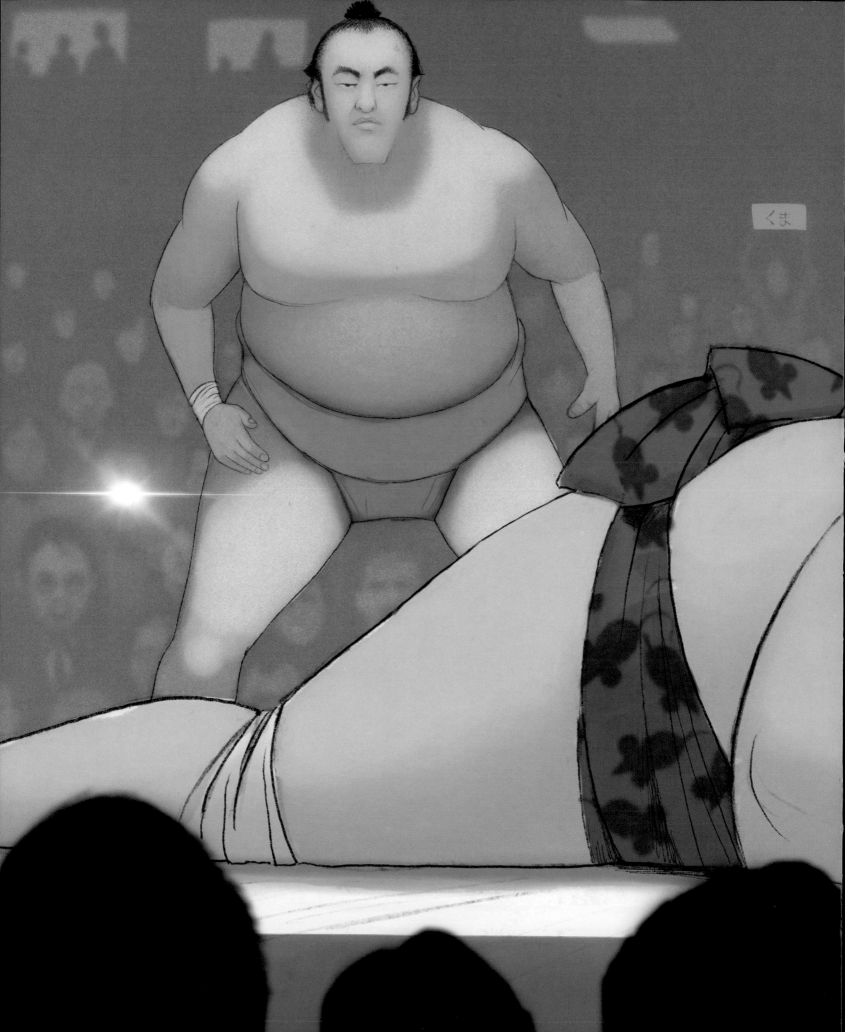

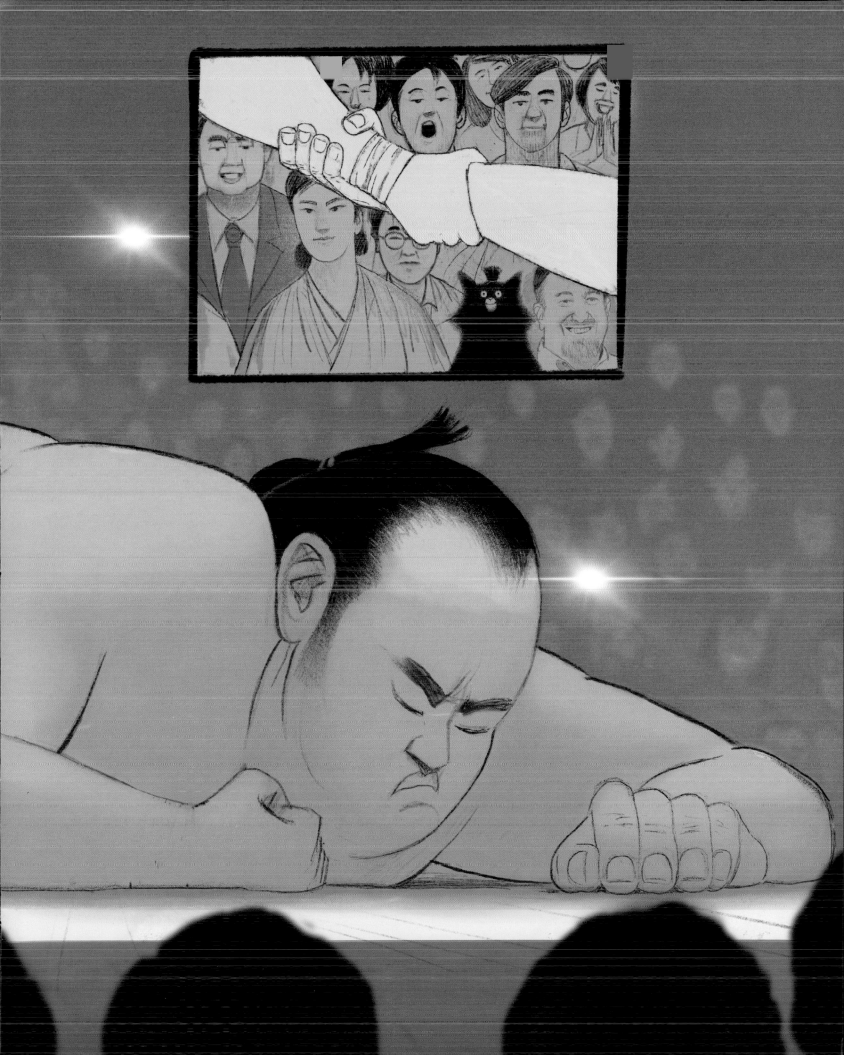

Now our heya has a new yokozuna picture hanging on the wall.

I might have had something to do with that.

And Kuma might have had something to do with me staying in the heya.

Fall down seven times; get up eight?

Purr-fect!

To Sox, the original SumoKitty